Inst System

SEASHORE STORY

By the same author

The Village Tree

Crow Boy

Umbrella

Youngest One

By Mitsu and Taro Yashima

Plenty to Watch

Momo's Kitten

SEASHORE STORY

Taro Yashima

THE VIKING PRESS   NEW YORK

First published in 1967 by The Viking Press, Inc. 625
Madison Avenue, New York, N.Y. 10022. Published
simultaneously in Canada by The Macmillan Company
of Canada Limited.

Library of Congress catalog card number: 66–11914
Printed in U.S.A. by Neff Lithographing Company.

Pic Bk 1. Japan—Stories

Trade 670–62710–0   VLB 670–62711–9

3   4   5   6   7   74   73   72   71   70

To
Frances Clarke Sayers
Vera Peterson
and
Sara Brant

Far away, on an island at the southern tip of Japan, is a seashore
where city noises never come at all.

The quietness of ancient times is there, just as it always was.

One day some children from a ballet school in a nearby town came to camp in the sand dunes there. The stillness of the beach reminded them of the old

familiar story of Urashima. "It could have happened here, in such a place," one said.

"Turtles come here too," another one said.

It is true that Urashima, the ancient fisherman of the story, was just like any of the fishermen who still live on this shore.

Urashima once saved the life of a wounded turtle just like the turtles that still come
to the shore to lay their eggs. And so the story begins.

A few days afterward the turtle swam up to Urashima's boat while he was fishing, as usual.

"Urashima! Urashima!" said the turtle. "Get on my back and I will take you to a beautiful place under the sea."

Urashima climbed on the turtle's back. And the turtle swam away into the depths of the ocean, leaving the shore far behind.

Day after day, night after night, the deep waters washed over them.

And at last they were in front of a huge gate like a mountain on the bottom of the sea.

Beyond, there rose a palace more grand than any Urashima had ever imagined
or dreamed of.

They glided within its walls, and found set before them a feast of strange, sweet-tasting food.

A procession of sea maidens danced before Urashima, the long seaweed sleeves of their kimonos swishing like foam.

Now day followed day, and night followed night. The happy time went on, and no one counted the days.

The deep sun-tan color of Urashima's face was no more.

Then one day Urashima suddenly remembered sun, and warm earth,
and his own people at home. He felt a great longing for them.

The sea people gave him a beautiful lacquered box as a farewell gift.

Once again the turtle and Urashima had a long journey through the deep sea.

And once again on the seashore where they had first met, the turtle said good-by to Urashima.

But when Urashima turned to the village and his home, there was not one face that he knew, not one house that was familiar.

Where was his own house? Gone. And his family, where were they?
No one knew of them, or even remembered.

He climbed up the mountain, the only place that looked the same to him, to open his precious box.

But from the box, only a thin line of white smoke arose. And at that moment, they say, Urashima became a white-haired old man.

Well, there it was. That was the end of the tale.

That was the story of Urashima the fisherman.

The children on the sand dunes were still talking about it. "Wasn't Urashima a good man?" one said.

"Yes, that is why he was so happy under the sea."

"Was there really a palace at the bottom of the sea?" asked another.
"Well, that was the way the ancient people believed."

"Then why had his house disappeared?" Suddenly a silent one spoke up. "And why his family gone? And why did only smoke come out of the beautiful box?"

"Because he stayed away too long," answered a young teacher. "You must always come back in time. It would not happen if you did not forget the people you love."

The children thought about that for awhile, saying nothing.

Only the youngest ones were not satisfied. "Even so, something better should have come out of a beautiful box."

"Yes, something much, much better. . . ."

The breeze from far over the ocean blew the children's voices into the sky.

Even the clouds seemed to be listening.

The sun that had warmed them touched the horizon and its last rays
rested on the children.

The soft sound of the waves told the end of the day.